Minton Goes!

SAILING

Anna Fienberg and Kim Gamble

ALLEN & UNWIN

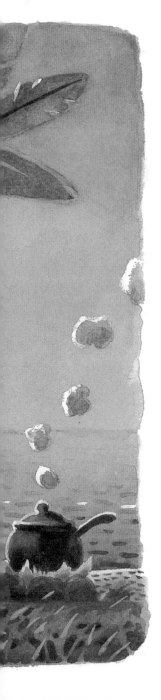

Minton was a beachcombing salamander. He slept in a hammock under the stars and cooked his dinner on a barbecue.

'What'll it be tonight?' he asked himself, as he looked out at the darkening ocean. 'Hmm, my favourite snack, I think – crispy roasted worms with beetle sauce.'

Every morning Minton took his bucket and hurried down to the shore to see what the waves had washed up.

'The sea brings us everything we need,' he told his best friend, Turtle.

It was the sea that brought him the wood to make his toolbox. Inside he put his hammer and nails, scissors and glue, and anything else he might need.

Minton liked the beach life. And he loved to make things. But he also wanted to explore.

'Who do you think lives on that island over there?' Minton asked Turtle one day.

'A monster that eats rocks? No one I'd like to meet, that's for sure,' said Turtle.

'Well,' said Minton, 'one day I will sail over and see. I am going to make a boat, and travel the world.'

'You'd better make anti-monster armour then, too,' snorted Turtle.

Minton had to wait almost a week before the sea brought him the first thing he needed.

'Bingo!' he cried. 'Here is the hull of my boat.' He opened his toolbox and took out his paints.

'It'll never float,' said Turtle. 'You'll sink like a rock and the monster will get you.'

'Bingo! Here is the mast of my boat.' Minton opened his toolbox and pulled out a piece of cork.

'It'll break,' said Turtle. 'First wave that comes along. You'll be somebody's breakfast.'

'Bingo! Here is my sail.' Minton took some string from his toolbox.

'Yuk!' said Turtle. 'Who knows what's been in that bag? Old fish bones and slimy sandwiches, I bet.'

Minton finished making his boat at sunset. That night, after his dinner of centipede stew, he laid out all the things he would need on his journey. He packed his towel, his torch, his life-jacket and toolbox neatly into the boat, ready for the morning.

He was so excited he wriggled and jiggled in his hammock. Then he lay awake looking at the stars, wondering if they would look different when he was on the island.

'You're not really going, are you?' asked Turtle.

'I certainly am,' said Minton. 'Are you coming?'

Turtle sighed. 'I suppose I'd better. After all, *I* wear anti-monster armour on my back. You'll see, I'll come dashing to save you, as usual.'

Minton sang as they cruised along. Seagulls flapped above, little waves licked gently at the boat below.

'This is the only way to travel, eh, Turtle?' said Minton.

Suddenly the sail ballooned with a fresh breeze and the boat began to zip along, scudding over the waves.

'We'll have to turn about if we're ever going to set foot on land again,' said Turtle.

But as they were turning, a blast of wind tipped them right over, and Minton and Turtle fell into the sea.

'Keep your eyes open for monsters!' Turtle managed to shout before they sank under the waves. A long dark shape flashed past, like a black arrow.

Minton and Turtle swam fast underwater, popping up to the surface like corks. They saw the boat lying on its side.

'Take the anchor rope, Turtle,' said Minton.
'There's only one thing for it — you'll have to tow us
to the island.'

Turtle took the rope in his mouth and began a
slow, told-you-so stroke with his flippers.

When they arrived at the island, Minton and Turtle pulled the boat up onto the sand.

They plunged into the jungle, Minton hacking at the vines with his saw.

Turtle took a deep breath. 'Perfume!' he said. 'These flowers smell good enough to eat.'

Minton popped a golden berry into his mouth. Honey spilled over his tongue. 'Delicious! This is a treasure island.'

Turtle watched Minton carefully to make sure the golden berries weren't poisonous. Then he helped pick a pile and they sat down to eat their lunch.

Suddenly there was a loud *thump thump* close by.

'The rock-eating monster!' cried Turtle.

Leaves crunched and a bush behind them shook. Something groaned. Minton jumped with fright.

The branches were pushed apart and a face peeped out.

'Sizzling somersaults! I'm glad to see you two.'

A tiny girl stepped towards them with her hand outstretched. 'I'm Bouncer the acrobat,' she said, 'and I'm tired of talking to plants.'

'Hello,' said Minton. 'What is an acrobat doing on this island?'

'Trying to bounce again,' she replied.

Bouncer did a cartwheel, landing neatly at Turtle's feet.

'I used to work in a circus, very far away. I cold do the highest jumps. But one day I couldn't stop. I did such a high jump, such a gigantic, enormous jump, that I flew over the city, over the farms and valleys, over the sea until I landed – plop! – right here on this island. And now I have no bounce left at all.'

'But don't you like it here?' asked Minton. 'You can eat these honeypot berries, and Turtle and I can visit you in our boat.'

Bouncer sighed. 'I miss the circus. I miss all my cousins and brothers and sisters and friends who live there. And I won't see them ever again!'

Minton stroked Bouncer's hand.

'I've never been to the circus,' he said softly. He looked out at the horizon, thinking. 'It would probably take too long to go to the other side of the world in my boat. I suppose we'll just have to build an aeroplane.'

'Cadoodling cartwheels!' cheered Bouncer. 'When do we start?'

'It'll never work,' said Turtle. 'You'll drop like a stone into the sea, and the killer whales will eat you.'

But Minton was already hurrying down to the shore to see what the sea would bring.

How to make Minton's boat

To make Minton's boat you'll need: a margarine or butter tub, 3 bamboo skewers, 2 corks, string, a plastic bag, scissors or sharp knife, tape or glue, and paint.

1. Trim tub to shape, and paint

2. Cut cork

3. Assemble mast (note, lower spar is longer than top spar)

The more weight in your boat the better it will sail.

4. Attach mast to boat, sprit at front goes into bottom cork. Secure with string. Cut sail to size and attach

Minton Goes!

FLYING

Minton walked along the shore, humming. He was going to make an aeroplane. He could see it all in his mind. He lifted some seaweed with his stick, and found just what he needed.

'Bingo! This will be the body of my plane.'

Turtle, Minton's friend came by. 'I wouldn't bother if I were you,' he said. 'What if there's a storm and you get struck by lightning? You'll *explode!*'

Bouncer the acrobat dashed up to them. 'I found this under my berry bush this morning. And I thought, maybe Minton can use it.'

'Bingo! Thanks, Bouncer, that will be the tail of my plane!'

Bouncer did a double somersault in the sand. She couldn't wait to get into that aeroplane and fly straight back to the circus. This island was very relaxing, but she missed the clowns and the animals and her family.

Minton took some masking tape and pins from his toolbox.

'What if a monster wind blows up?' said Turtle. 'We'll be blown right out of the sky.'

'Is he always like this?' asked Bouncer.

'Pretty much,' said Minton. 'But he is very brave.'

Minton found some good
strong cardboard in his toolbox
for the wings, and he cut them
out with his scissors. Bouncer
helped him stick them on, and
then they mixed up some paints.

Minton was just fixing the
cockpit when a couple of
seagulls flew by.

'Hey, Minton!' they
squawked. 'Need these for your
plane?'

'Bingo!' cried Minton. 'Here
are my jet engines!'

By the end of the day the aeroplane was ready.

'It's aerodynamic!' cheered Bouncer.

'It's supersonic!' cried Minton.

'It will be the end of us,' said Turtle.

Minton marked out a runway in the sand with his stick. Turtle crushed berries to make juice for the petrol. This took a while because he kept eating the berries.

Finally they were ready. Minton and Turtle climbed into the aeroplane and Bouncer, who was the fastest runner, gave them a push from behind. As they rose up into the air, Bouncer did a double backflip with a half twist and landed in the plane.

The night sky was soft with moonlight. Minton looked at the stars with his telescope. The three friends smiled at each other, way up there in the sky.

But clouds passed over the moon and a cool
wind sprang up.

'Hang on,' said Minton. 'We're in for a bit of
rough weather.'

The wind howled, tearing and tugging at the wings. The plane shot up and down like a ball as the wind threw it around the sky.

Minton gripped the steering wheel. Bouncer felt her stomach sink, as if she were zooming down too fast from a high jump.

'The monster wind! I knew it,' moaned Turtle, and slid back into his shell.

And then a mighty gust blew
Bouncer right out of the plane.
She grabbed onto the wing, her
legs streaming behind her like
two ribbons in the wind.

'Can you hang on?' called
Minton.

'I'm trying,' called Bouncer.
'It's like swinging on the
tightrope at the circus.
Only…much…harder!'

Turtle's head popped out of his shell.

'Minton,' he said, 'I'll lean over the side of the plane. You crawl across my shell and reach out to Bouncer. I'll stop you from falling.'

'But won't *you* fall?'

'Help, I'm slipping!' called Bouncer.

Minton scrambled over Turtle and stretched out his arm as far as it would go. Bouncer grasped it with one hand, then two. Minton pulled. Bouncer clung. Turtle grunted.

Then Bouncer was back inside the plane.

'Phew! That was close,' said Bouncer. 'Thanks for saving me!'

'What are friends for?' said Turtle.

As the wind died down to a gentle sigh, the three friends gazed out into the dark, glad to be safe together.

When the sun rose, they saw a farm down below, with cows munching on fields of green. They passed over rivers and valleys and hills. And then they saw the city.

'I'm home!' cried Bouncer. She pointed to a clearing in the middle of some tall buildings. On the grass sat a big orange tent.

They glided in, right in front of the tent.
Acrobats and dancers came running and leaping.
Clowns on shoes as long as fence posts tumbled
towards them.

'*Bouncer!*' they called, and the jugglers dropped
their balls and the dancers forgot their steps as they
caught her in their arms and wrapped her in hugs.

That night Minton and Turtle sat in the front row of the circus. There was a roll of drums. A single spotlight shone on Bouncer. The audience held its breath.

Then Bouncer took a giant leap and flew like a firecracker over their heads. In mid-air she curled into a somersault and came whirling down on the other side. The audience clapped like thunder.

'Lucky there's a roof on this tent,' said Turtle. 'A girl like her, she'd bounce up to the moon is she wasn't careful.'

After the show, Bouncer took Minton and Turtle to meet her family.

'You know, I like it here in the city,' said Minton.

'Oh yes, and there's so much more to do,' said Bouncer. 'There are swings and slides and pony rides…'

'Well, we'll need a car to zip around in then, won't we,' said Minton thoughtfully.

'Walking is safer,' sighed Turtle.

But Minton was already wondering what he could use to make his wheels.

'Toot toot,' he said softly to himself.

'Uh oh,' said Turtle.

How to make Minton's plane

To make Minton's plane you'll need:

a plastic bottle, 2 toilet rolls, masking tape, cardboard approx. 50cm x 15cm, scissors or sharp knife, and paint

cut

cut

cut

cut

50cm

15cm

1. Cut out windscreen, and make slots as shown

2. Cut out wing and tail

3. Attach windscreen with tape as shown

4. Slide wing into place and secure with tape. Repeat for tail. Attach engine tubes. Paint

Happy flying!